A Stick Until...

Constance Anderson

STAR BRIGHT BOOKS

CAMBRIDGE MASSACHUSETTS

The name Star Bright Books and the Star Bright Books logo are registered
trademarks of Star Bright Books, Inc. Please visit: www.starbrightbooks.com.
For bulk orders, please email: orders@starbrightbooks.com, or call customer
service at: (617) 354-1300.

Printed on paper from sustainable forests.

Hardback ISBN-13: 978-1-59572-777-0
Paperback ISBN-13: 978-1-59572-778-7
Star Bright Books / MA / 00104170
Printed in China / WKT / 9 8 7 6 5 4 3 2 1

Library of Congress Cataloging-in-Publication Data is available.

To Tristan and Travis, childhood masters of inventive, inspiring stick use. And to Alan for making it so.

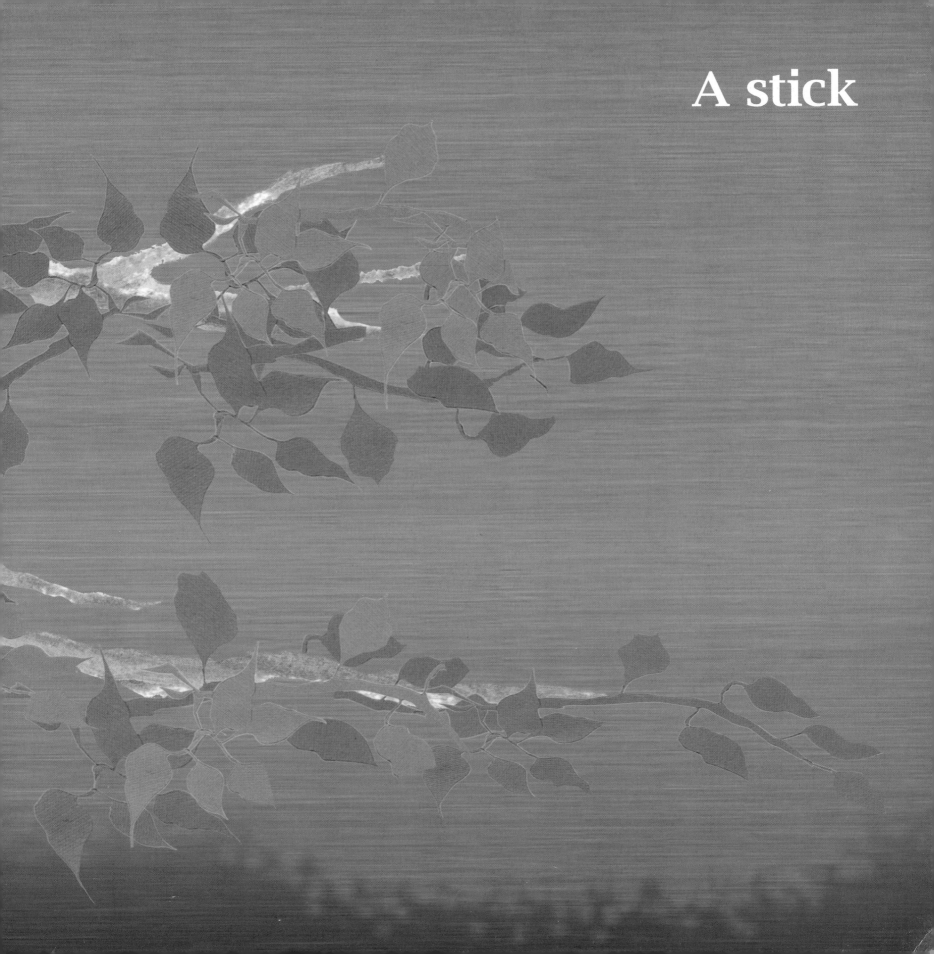

A stick

is a branch of a tree until . . .

it is a flyswatter. It is a flyswatter until . . .

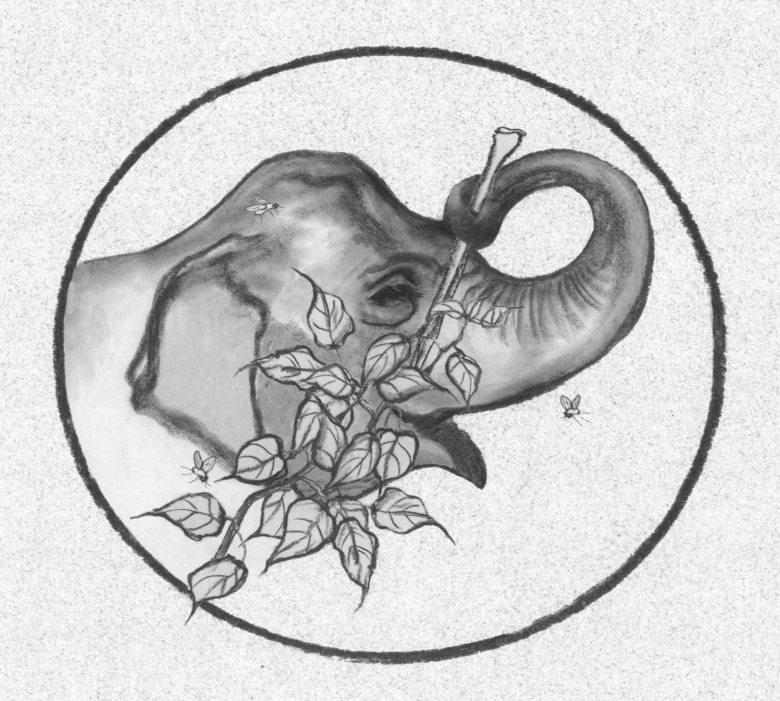

*The Asian elephant breaks off a tree branch
to swat the pesky flies that bite its tough skin.*

it is a walking cane.

It is a walking cane until . . .

A gorilla in a Congolese forest tests the depth of muddy water with a stick. Then she uses the stick as a walking cane to cross the marsh.

it is a spoon.

Chimpanzees spoon termites into their mouths with a stick.
Termites are insects and one of chimpanzees' favorite snacks.

To dig into a termite mound, chimpanzees use different sticks. They pierce the mound with a stout stick, then use a long, slender stick to fish inside for termites.

it is bait.

Partially submerged alligators balance sticks on top of their long snouts during the bird breeding season of herons and egrets. The sticks look like they are floating in the water.

It is bait until . . .

A bird searching for sticks to build a nest might be caught by an alligator if it takes the bait.

it is a gift,

The male great egret presents a stick to the female as a gift, and if she accepts it, they make a nest together.

a gift until . . .

Great egrets get to know each other during mating season by stretching and displaying their graceful breeding plumage.

it is part of a nest.

The female great egret lays 3-5 blue eggs and both parents take turns feeding their young.

A stick is part of a nest until . . .

They make platform nests out of sticks high above ground or water, nesting in colonies with other herons.

a winter storm blows it far away.

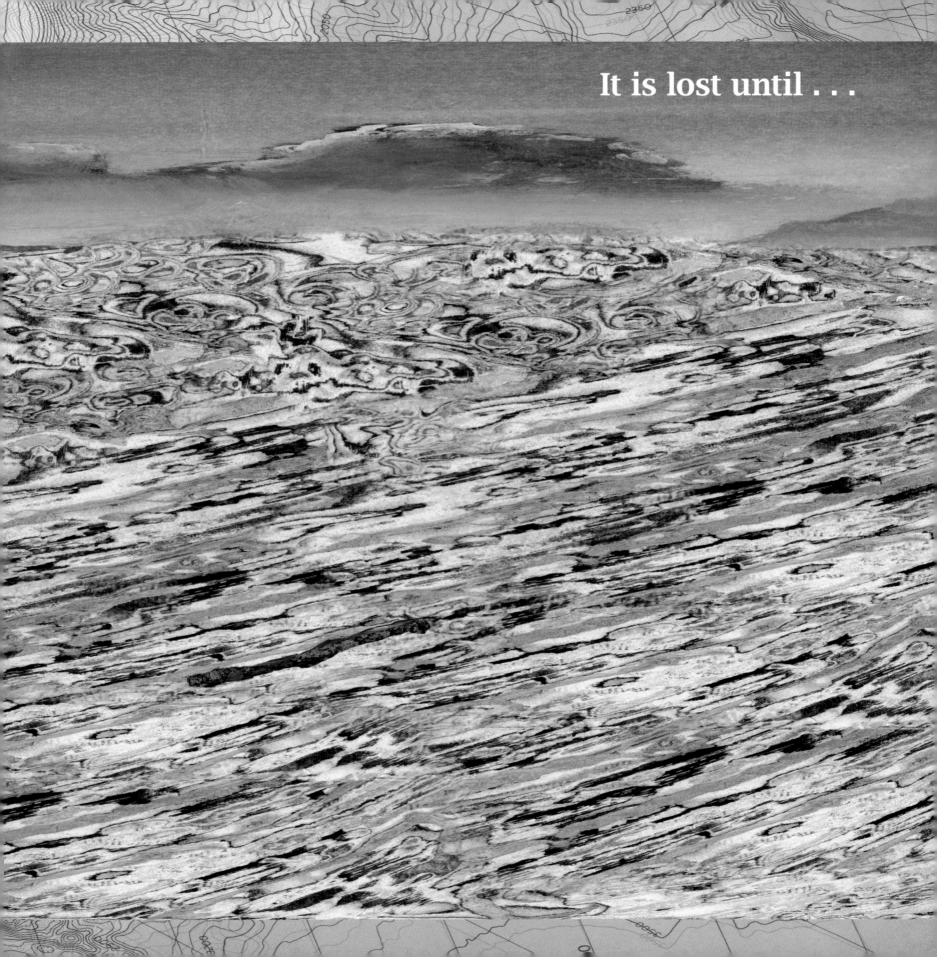

It is lost until . . .

it is found.

A stick is used to play a game,

*Throw a stick to a dog and the game begins. Prey drive is
the instinct that makes dogs want to track, find, and fetch.*

Ready, set, go! Hoop rolling, running alongside a rolling wheel while keeping it upright with a stick, is a game played all over the world.

it inspires make believe,

helps draw a picture,

dig a hole,

and supports a sapling that grows

to be a home.

Notes

Elephants and Flyswatters

Elephants are healthier when parasitic flies are kept away. The biting flies cause pain and blood loss, and often pass on disease. After an elephant finds a branch, it shapes it by tearing off unnecessary limbs, making it just right for swatting. Elephants also use their tails to swat flies.

Chimpanzees and Spoons

Anthropologist Dr. Jane Goodall was the first person to notice the use of a stick by an African chimpanzee to fish for and eat termites. Before her observation in 1960, at Gombe National Park in Tanzania, Africa, it was thought that animals did not use tools.

Gorillas, Walking Canes, and Bridges

In addition to using sticks as walking canes, gorillas in Africa make bridges out them. Gorillas find tree and shrub branches, pile them up, and walk over the bridge that spans a marsh or pond.

Alligators Nests

Like birds, alligators make nests and lay eggs. Their onshore nests are made of muddy vegetation and branches. Nests often measure up to 6 feet wide and 3 feet high. A mother alligator lays 20-50 eggs. After 65 days, the hatchlings break out of their shells and head for water, their 6-9 inch bodies camouflaged by a yellow stripe.

Herons and Hats

Because the elegant breeding plumes of egrets were fashionable in women's hats in the late 1800's, egret populations were threatened. Harriet Hemenway and her cousin, Minna Hall, refused to buy the hats and asked their friends to do the same. They set off a revolt that resulted in laws protecting the birds. Their movement led to one of the first environmental organizations, The National Audubon Society. The great egret, once almost hunted to extinction but saved by conservation efforts, is the symbol of the National Audubon Society.

Dogs and Drive

Like their ancestor the wolf, dogs have a prey instinct. The prey instinct is the urge to seek out, pursue, and capture prey. Prehistoric people saw how effective dogs were in tracking and catching prey so they domesticated dogs to help them hunt food. Today, dogs exhibit their prey drive when they chase and fetch sticks.

Hoop Rolling Games

Hoop rolling games have been played with metal hoops, wooden hoops, and old bicycle tires. Here are some hoop rolling games.

Hoop race
From a starting point, hoop players run along and see who can keep the hoop rolling the furthest.

Last hoop standing
Players roll hoops toward each other, using their hoop to knock down as many other hoops as possible.

Turnpike
An obstacle course is set up. Players drive their hoop through pairs of objects placed on the ground, like stones or bricks. Whoever gets through without hitting the objects wins.